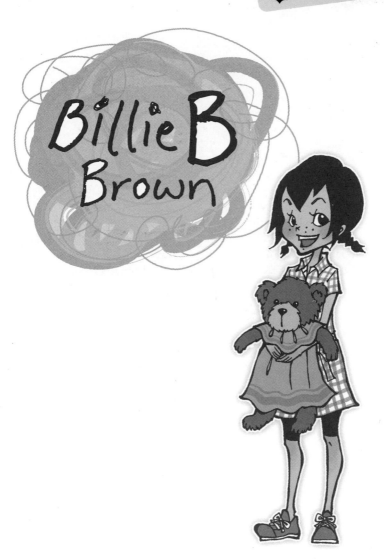

Billie B Brown

www.BillieBBrown.com

The Big Sister
published in 2012 by
Hardie Grant Egmont
Ground Floor, Building 1, 658 Church Street
Richmond, Victoria 3121, Australia
www.hardiegrantegmont.com.au

A CiP record for this title is available from the National Library of Australia

Text copyright © 2012 Sally Rippin
Illustration copyright © 2012 Aki Fukuoka
Logo and design copyright © 2012 Hardie Grant Egmont

Design and typeset by Stephanie Spartels

Printed in China by Everbest Printing Co.

The Big Sister

By Sally Rippin

Illustrated by Aki Fukuoka

hardie grant EGMONT

Chapter One

Billie B Brown has four baby jumpsuits, three tiny dresses and one big teddy bear. Do you know what the B in Billie B Brown stands for?

Baby!

Billie's mum is having a baby. Billie is going to be a big sister!

These little clothes used to be Billie's. Aren't they tiny? They will be perfect for the new baby.

Billie is very **excited** about being a big sister.

Four baby
jumpsuits

Three tiny dresses

One big
teddy bear

3

She's going to give the baby her favourite teddy, Mr Fred. Isn't that nice of her?

Billie has had Mr Fred since she was a baby. But when the baby comes she won't need him anymore.

Today Billie is playing mummies and daddies with her best friend, Jack.

Jack lives next door.
Billie and Jack have
been friends since they
were little. They do
everything together.

Billie and Jack sit in the
cubby they have made.
Billie squeezes Mr Fred
into a pink dress.
He looks very funny.
Billie and Jack giggle.

Today it is Jack's turn to
look after the baby while
Billie goes off to work.

'I'm glad you're home,' says Jack when Billie comes back. 'Mr Fred has been crying all day!'

Billie laughs and takes Mr Fred. 'I'm bored of playing mummies and daddies,' she says. 'Let's go and play soccer.'

Jack and Billie run into the garden to play.

Billie sits Mr Fred on the grass to watch.

Oh dear. Look at those grey clouds.

9

Soon it starts to rain.

Billie and Jack run inside.
But they forget someone.

Poor Mr Fred! He is
going to get very wet,
isn't he?

Chapter Two

That night, Billie's mum reads her a story in bed. It is about a mummy elephant and her baby. It is Billie's favourite book.

Suddenly Billie's mum stops reading. She gets a funny look on her face.

'Oh!' she says. 'I think the baby is coming!'

She calls to Billie's dad.

Billie climbs out of bed and helps her mum downstairs. Billie's dad rushes around finding all the things they will need for hospital.

Suddenly Billie gets a funny feeling in her tummy. 'Can I come with you?' she says.

'No, sweetheart,' says her dad. 'Remember, we said that you will stay at Jack's house when the baby comes.'

'How long will you be?' asks Billie, feeling **worried**.

'I don't know, Billie,' says her mum.

She squeezes Billie's hand.
'But just think — next
time you see me, you will
have a little baby brother
or sister!'

But Billie has decided
she doesn't want a silly
old baby anymore.
She wants her mummy!
Billie scrunches up her
face and tries not to cry.

'It's all right, Billie,' says
her dad gently.

Jack's mum comes
over to pick up Billie.
They watch Billie's mum
and dad drive off.

Billie's mum blows a
kiss but Billie looks
down at the ground.
She doesn't want them to
go without her.

Jack's mum gives Billie a cuddle. 'I've made a bed for you in Jack's room,' she says. They walk next door.

Jack is already asleep. His mum tucks Billie into the spare bed.

Jack's room looks
strange in the dark.
Billie wishes she was
back in her own bed.

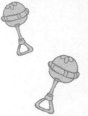

Suddenly she sits up.

'Mr Fred!' she whispers.
'I need Mr Fred!'

'Oh dear. We'll get
him tomorrow,' says
Jack's mum.

'How about you sleep
with one of Jack's toys
tonight?'

Jack's mum gives Billie
a big blue teddy bear.
He is very soft and cuddly.
But he's not like Mr Fred.

Billie lies in the dark.
Her tummy is curling up
with **worry**.

She can't remember
where she put Mr Fred!

You remember where he
is though, don't you?

Chapter Three

The next day, Billie
has breakfast with Jack's
family. But she doesn't
feel very hungry.

Just then there is a knock
on the door. It's Billie's dad!

'Billie!' he says excitedly. 'Guess what? You have a baby brother!'

'A brother?' Billie says, frowning. 'But I wanted a sister! Who will wear all my baby dresses now?'

'Oh, Billie,' says her dad, giving her a cuddle. 'You should see him.

He's beautiful! And I'm sure he'll look lovely in your pretty pink dresses.'

Billie giggles. 'Where's Mum?' she asks. 'Is she coming home now?'

'Not yet,' her dad says. 'Mum has to rest. She will be at the hospital for a few days. But we can go and see her.'

'A few days!' Billie says crossly. 'But I want Mum to come home now.' She **stamps** her foot.

Billie's dad sighs.

He thanks Jack's parents for looking after Billie. Billie and her dad go back home for Billie to get dressed.

Billie feels all jumbled up inside. She is **excited** to see her new baby brother. But she also feels a teensy bit **cross** that he is a boy, not a girl.

She is **excited** to see her mum, but she is also **cross** that her mum is not coming home yet. All these feelings bubble up inside Billie's tummy like a milkshake.

Then she remembers.

'Mr Fred!' she says.
'I have to find Mr Fred
to give to the new baby!'

'OK,' says her dad.
'But quickly. Mum is
waiting for us.'

Billie looks everywhere for
Mr Fred. She looks under
her bed. No Mr Fred.
Then she checks her
toy box. Not there either!

She checks all the
places Mr Fred could be.
But he is nowhere to
be found.

'We have to go now,'
Billie's dad says. 'We can
give Mr Fred to the baby
next time.'

'No!' says Billie. 'I want Mr Fred!' She **stamps** her feet.

'Billie!' says her dad. He is looking very tired. 'Come on. You have to be a big girl now.'

'But I don't want to be a big girl!' Billie cries. 'I want to be a baby too!'

Billie's dad bends down
and gives her a big hug.

'It's OK,' he says gently.
'You will always be my
baby girl, Billie. Now how
about we go see Mum?

We can look for Mr Fred again when we get home.'

Billie stops crying and gives her dad a big cuddle.

Chapter Four

Billie and her dad arrive
at the hospital. Her mum
is sitting up in bed.
She holds out her arms
and Billie jumps onto the
bed for a cuddle.

Billie's mum points to a plastic cot next to the bed. 'There's your little brother,' she says. 'His name is Noah. Isn't he adorable?'

Billie looks into the plastic cot. Noah is wrapped up like a fat white caterpillar. His face is all squishy and red. He doesn't look very adorable to Billie.

'Would you like a hold?' her mum asks.

'Nah,' says Billie, snuggling up to her mum. 'Maybe later.'

Billie's mum lets her change
the channels on the TV.
Then Billie tells her mum
about poor lost Mr Fred.

Soon it is time to go.
Billie kisses her mum
goodbye. She even gives
Noah a kiss. He smells nice.
Like banana pancakes!

'Bye-bye, baby!' Billie
says softly.

Just then Noah opens
his eyes. He looks
straight up at Billie.
A little smile creeps over
his tiny face. Then he
closes his eyes again.

'He smiled at me!'
Billie gasps.

'Wow, Billie! You're the
first person he's smiled
at,' her mum says.

'That's because he knows
you're his big sister,' her
dad says.

Billie feels very **proud**.
She is the first person her
baby brother has smiled at.

He likes her! Maybe it will be fun to be a big sister after all.

'OK, time to go,' says her dad. 'Let's go home and look for Mr Fred, shall we?'

When they get home, Jack is waiting on Billie's front doorstep.

He has something in
his arms. Something
big and furry and wet
and muddy.

'Mr Fred!' Billie says.

'Oh dear,' says her dad.
'Did you leave him out
in the rain?'

Billie nods. She gives poor
old Mr Fred a big cuddle.

She has missed him so much!

'I don't think I want to give Mr Fred to Noah anymore,' Billie says.

'After all, Mr Fred is a bit old and dirty for our new baby.'

Billie knows that being a big sister will be fun most days. But some days she might want to be a baby, too. She will need Mr Fred on those days.

'But what will you give the baby?' Jack asks.

Billie smiles. 'Our new baby needs a *new* teddy bear,' she says. 'Just for him!'

Then she giggles. 'And do you know what else? I think Mr Fred needs a bath!'

Collect them all!

1. The Bad Butterfly — By Sally Rippin
2. The Soccer Star — By Sally Rippin
3. The Second-best Friend — By Sally Rippin
4. The Midnight Feast — By Sally Rippin
5. The Beautiful Haircut — By Sally Rippin
6. The Extra-special Helper — By Sally Rippin
7. The Perfect Present — By Sally Rippin
8. The Secret Message — By Sally Rippin
9. The Big Sister — By Sally Rippin
10. The Birthday Mix-up — By Sally Rippin

Play cool games and leave a message for Billie at

www.BillieBBrown.com